LITTLE RED RIDING HOOD

AND OTHER GIRLS WHO GOT LOST IN THE WOODS

Amelia Carruthers

Origins of Fairy Tales from Around the World

Copyright © 2015 Pook Press
An imprint of Read Publishing Ltd.
Home Farm, 44 Evesham Road, Cookhill, Alcester,
Warwickshire, B49 5LJ

Introduced and edited by Amelia Carruthers.
Cover design by Zoë Horn Haywood.
Design by Zoë Horn Haywood and Sam Bigland.

British Library Cataloguing-in-Publication Data. A catalogue record for this book is available from the British Library.

CONTENTS

An Introduction to

the Fairy Tale

Fairy Tales are told in almost every society, all over the globe. They have the ability to inspire generations of young and old alike, yet fail to fit neatly into any one mode of storytelling. Today, most people know these narratives through literary works or even film versions, but this is a far cry from the genre's early development. Most of the stories began, and are still propagated through oral traditions, which are still very much alive in certain cultures. Especially in rural, poorer regions, the telling of tales – from village to village, or from elder to younger, preserves culture and custom, whilst still enabling the teller to vary, embellish or adapt the tale as they see fit.

To provide a brief attempt at definition, a fairy tale is a type of short story that typically features 'fantasy' characters, such as dwarves, elves, fairies, giants, gnomes, goblins, mermaids, trolls or witches, and usually magic or enchantments to boot! Fairy tales may be distinguished from other folk narratives such as legends (which generally involve belief in the veracity of the events described) and explicitly moral tales, including fables or those of a religious nature. In cultures where demons and witches are perceived as real, fairy tales may merge into legends, where the narrative is perceived both by teller and hearers as being grounded in historical truth. However unlike legends and epics, they usually do not contain more than superficial references to religion and actual places, people, and events; they take place 'once upon a time' rather than in reality.

The history of the fairy tale is particularly difficult to trace, as most often, it is only the literary forms that are available to the scholar. Still, written evidence indicates that fairy tales have existed for thousands of years, although not perhaps recognized as a genre. Many of today's fairy narratives have evolved from centuries-old stories that have appeared, with variations, in multiple cultures around the world. Two theories of origins have attempted to explain the common elements in fairy tales across continents. One is that a single point of origin generated any given tale, which then spread over the centuries. The other is that such fairy tales stem from common human experience and therefore can appear separately in many different origins. Debates still rage over which interpretation is correct, but as ever, it is likely that a combination of both aspects are involved in the advancements of these folkloric chronicles.

Some folklorists prefer to use the German term *Märchen* or 'wonder tale' to refer to the genre over *fairy tale,* a practice given weight by the definition of Thompson in his 1977 edition of *The Folktale.* He described it as 'a tale of some length involving a succession of motifs or episodes. It moves in an unreal world without definite locality or definite creatures and is filled with the marvellous. In this never-never land, humble heroes kill adversaries, succeed to kingdoms and marry princesses.' The genre was first marked out by writers of the Renaissance, such as Giovanni Francesco Straparola and Giambattista Basile, and stabilized through the works of later collectors such as Charles Perrault and the Brothers Grimm. The oral tradition of the fairy tale came long before the written page however.

Tales were told or enacted dramatically, rather than written down, and handed from generation to generation. Because of this, many fairy tales appear in written literature throughout different cultures, as in *The Golden Ass*, which includes *Cupid and Psyche* (Roman, 100–200 CE), or the *Panchatantra* (India, 3rd century CE). However it is still unknown to what extent these reflect the actual folk tales even of their own time. The 'fairy tale' as a genre became popular among the French nobility of the seventeenth century, and among the tales told were the *Contes* of Charles Perrault (1697), who fixed the forms of 'Sleeping Beauty' and 'Cinderella.' Perrault largely laid the foundations for this new literary variety, with some of the best of his works including 'Puss in Boots', 'Little Red Riding Hood' and 'Bluebeard'.

The first collectors to attempt to preserve not only the plot and characters of the tale, but also the style in which they were told were the Brothers Grimm, who assembled German fairy tales. The Brothers Grimm rejected several tales for their anthology, though told by Germans, because the tales derived from Perrault and they concluded that the stories were thereby *French* and not *German* tales. An oral version of 'Bluebeard' was thus rejected, and the tale of 'Little Briar Rose', clearly related to Perrault's 'The Sleeping Beauty' was included only because Jacob Grimm convinced his brother that the figure of *Brynhildr*, from much earlier Norse mythology, proved that the sleeping princess was authentically German. The Grimm Brothers remain some of the best-known story-tellers of folk tales though, popularising 'Hansel and Gretel', 'Rapunzel', 'Rumplestiltskin' and 'Snow White.'

The work of the Brothers Grimm influenced other collectors, both inspiring them to collect tales and leading them to similarly believe, in a spirit of romantic nationalism, that the fairy tales of a country were particularly representative of it (unfortunately generally ignoring any cross-cultural references). Among those influenced were the Norwegian Peter Christen Asbjørnsen (*Norske Folkeeventyr*, 1842-3), the Russian Alexander Afanasyev (*Narodnye Russkie Skazki*, 1855-63) and the Englishman, Joseph Jacobs (*English Fairy Tales*, 1890). Simultaneously to such developments, writers such as Hans Christian Andersen and George MacDonald continued the tradition of penning original literary fairy tales. Andersen's work sometimes drew on old folktales, but more often deployed fairytale motifs and plots in new stories; for instance in 'The Little Mermaid', 'The Ugly Duckling' and 'The Emperor's New Clothes.'

Fairy tales are still written in the present day, attesting to their enormous popularity and cultural longevity. Aside from their long and diverse literary history, these stories have also been stunningly illustrated by some of the world's best artists – as the reader will be able to see in the following pages. The Golden Age of Illustration (a period customarily defined as lasting from the latter quarter of the nineteenth century until just after the First World War) produced some of the finest examples of this craft, and the masters of the trade are all collected in this volume, alongside the original, inspiring tales. These images form their own story, evolving in conjunction with the literary development of the tales. Consequently, the illustrations are presented in their own narrative sequence, for the reader to appreciate *in and of themselves*. An introduction to the 'Golden Age' can also be found at the end of this book.

THE HISTORY OF
LITTLE RED RIDING HOOD

Little Red Riding Hood is one of the world's best known fairy tales, and provides the name for the tale type classified as Aarne-Thompson index; no.333. Despite its ubiquity in the modern day, as fairy tales go, *Little Red Riding Hood* has a relatively short history. It is a European folktale, first written down in the form we know today in the seventeenth century. Most scholars date the first 'fixed' version as Charles Perrault's *Le Petit Chaperon Rouge* (1697), with the Brothers Grimm providing a slightly differing account in *Kinder und Hausmärchen* ('Children's and Household Tales') in 1812. Yet despite these 'modern' beginnings, it is possible to trace a far longer lineage of the narrative form. At its core, the story involves a young girl (generally walking in a forest, wearing a red cap or cape) who, at some point, encounters a *big bad wolf* character.

The theme of a ravening creature, and a person released unharmed from its belly is prevalent in many other tales; most famously in the biblical story of *Jonah and the Whale,* as well as in the story of Saint Margaret, where the saint emerges unharmed from the belly of a dragon. A similar narrative is also evidenced in the character of Cronus in Hesiod's tales (700 BCE), who swallows then disgorges his children alive. Aside from such broad themes, the direct origins of the *Little Red Riding Hood* Story can be discovered in accounts told by French and Italian peasants in the tenth and fourteenth centuries. Whilst very few of these were written down in their full form, there is a version noted by the French folklorist Achille Millien of an Italian form named *La Finta Nonna* ('The False Grandmother'). The story recounts the rather gruesome tale of a girl's encounter with a wolf (who has killed her grandmother), who then feeds the young lady her grandmother's blood and flesh. The girl only manages to escape by excusing herself to go to the bathroom.

Whilst this story has very obvious similarities to the version of *Little Red Riding Hood* we know today, some have argued that the tale has had a far wider geographical reach, with examples found in China from the Quing Dynasty (1644-1912), most notably the narrative of 'Grandaunt Tiger.' In this variant, a panther or a tiger (in a similar manner to the 'wolf' creature) persuades the children to let her in the house, claiming to be a grandaunt or grandmother. These early variations of the tale differ from today's popular narrative in several ways. The antagonist is not always a wolf, but sometimes an ogre or a 'bzou' (werewolf), and the unwitting cannibalization evidenced in the early Italian version disappears in later, slightly bowdlerised variants. Interestingly in these stories, the young girl escapes without any help from an older male or female figure (in most cases *the huntsman*), instead using her own cunning.

Having said this, some scholars have argued that *Little Red Riding Hood* in fact originates from a far simpler tale, that of 'The Wolf In Sheep's Clothing', which appears in *Aesop's Fables*. Aesop (who lived in ancient Greece between 620 and 560 BCE) describes a wolf that resolves 'to disguise his appearance in order to secure food more easily' but on meeting an untimely end, provides the moral of 'Harm seek. Harm find.' The harm met by Aesop's wolf is not matched in Perrault's 1697 version (in which the young girl remains unsaved), but is reflected in the Brothers Grimm's *Rotkäppchen*, where the huntsman rescues the grandmother and the girl by cutting open the wolf's belly with a pair of scissors.

Such was the consternation over these differing endings, that Andrew Lang (an English story-teller) explicitly stated in his version that the tale had been previously mis-told. In his variant, *The True History of Little Goldenhood* (1890), the girl is saved not by the huntsman, but by her own hood. As with all folkloric stories, the origins are mixed, but Lang most likely derived his tale from another French author, Charles Marelles.

Although Perrault's ending differs considerably from Aesop's original tale, the French author still felt that his story contained an obvious moral. From the narrative one learns that children (especially young ladies) do very wrong to listen to strangers and that it is not unheard of, if the 'wolf' is thereby provided with his dinner. These wolves represented the men of Paris, who innocent young girls should avoid; 'I say Wolf, for all wolves are not of the same sort; there is one kind with an amenable disposition – neither noisy, nor hateful, nor angry, but tame, obliging and gentle, following the young maids in the streets, even into their homes. Alas! Who does not know that these gentle wolves are of all such creatures the most dangerous!' The sexual overtones of the story would not have been lost on contemporary readers, as the French idiom for a girl having lost her virginity was 'elle avoit vû le loup' (*she has seen the wolf*). In many of *Little Red Riding Hood's* other variants however, the tale is merely meant to instill a general terror in young children of 'the beast' – with the narrator traditionally meant to make a pounce, in the character of the wolf, at their youngest listener.

As a testament to this storie's ability to inspire and entertain generations of readers, *Little Red Riding Hood* continues to influence popular culture internationally, lending plot elements, allusions, and tropes to a wide variety of artistic mediums. It has been translated into almost every language, and very excitingly, is continuing to evolve in the present day. We hope the reader enjoys this collection of some of its best re-tellings.

Once upon a time, there lived in a certain village, a little country girl.
Tales of Passed Times, 1900.
Illustrated by John Austen

The Wolf in Sheep's Clothing

(A Greek Tale)

Although very obviously different from the modern versions of *Little Red Riding Hood* (there being no little girl, and no red hood), Aesop's fable can be seen as the very first written example of the 'threatening wolf character.' In a comparable manner to later variants, where the *big bad wolf* disguises his appearance as the grandmother, Aesop's wolf dresses as a sheep. As well as this, Aesop's unfortunate ending for the wolf and the subsequent moral lesson, is replicated in the Brothers Grimm's telling, where their wolf meets a similarly gruesome end.

Aesop was an Ancient Greek slave and story teller thought to have lived between 620 and 564 BCE. Scattered details of Aesop's life can be found in ancient sources, including Aristotle, Herodotus, and Plutarch, but fittingly for the fairy tale genre, most are episodic probably highly fictional accounts of his life. Although his existence remains uncertain and (if he ever existed) no writings by him survive, numerous tales credited to him were gathered across the centuries in many languages – in a storytelling tradition that continues to this day.

➤——→

Once upon a time a Wolf resolved to disguise his appearance in order to secure food more easily. Encased in the skin of a sheep, he pastured with the flock deceiving the shepherd by his costume. In the evening he was shut up by the shepherd in the fold; the gate was closed, and the entrance made thoroughly secure. But the shepherd, returning to the fold during the night to obtain meat for the next day, mistakenly caught up the Wolf instead of a sheep, and killed him instantly. Harm seek. Harm find.

Take her this cake and this little pot of butter.
Little Red Riding Hood & the History of Tom Thumb, 1895.
Illustrated by H. Isabel Adams

THE FALSE GRANDMOTHER

(An Italian Tale)

This story, although published in 1887 by the Frenchman Achille Millien (1838 - 1927) is an example of one of the earliest tellings of the *Little Red Riding Hood* narrative as we know it today. Known as *La Finta Nonna* ('The False Grandmother'), it was traditionally recounted by fourteenth century peasants living in Abruzzo, a region of Southern Italy which boasts the title of the 'Greenest Region in Europe' – *and lots of woods.*

Unlike later variations of the tale, the protagonist is invited to eat her grandmother's flesh and blood (which she does so unwittingly), and only manages to escape by pretending to need the bathroom. Some oral versions of the tale present several girls rather than one, for instance, *Il Lupo e le Tre Ragazze* ('The Wolf and the Three Girls'), a formulation later popularised by the Brothers Grimm's *Wolf and the Seven Young Kids* (1812).

>——→

Once upon a time a girl was walking through the woods with a basket of goodies for her grandmother, when she met a wolf.

"Good day," said the wolf. "Where are you going so early in the morning?"

Now the girl did not know that the wolf was a wicked animal, so she told him that she was going to visit her grandmother, who lived on the other side of the woods. She continued merrily on her way. The wicked wolf ran on ahead and arrived at the grandmother's house before the girl. He crept inside, leaped on the poor grandmother, and ate her up, saving only a pitcher of blood and a piece of flesh. He then climbed into the grandmother's bed, and waited for the girl. The girl soon arrived, and knocked at the door.

"Just let yourself in," said the wolf, disguising his voice. "You must be hungry from your long walk through the woods. Do eat some of the meat that's on the kitchen table."

And the girl ate from her grandmother's flesh.

"You must be thirsty from your long walk through the woods. Do drink from the pitcher that's on the kitchen table."

And the girl drank from her grandmother's blood.

"You must be tired from your long walk through the woods. Do come to bed with me."

And the girl climbed into bed with the wolf.

She soon saw that it was not her grandmother in the bed with her, and she became frightened. Not knowing how else to escape, she said, "I have to go to the privy."

"You can just do it in the bed," answered the wicked wolf.

"I don't have to go little. I have to go big," said the girl.

"All right," said the wolf, "but hurry right back as soon as you are done."

The girl ran out of the house, and she ran past the privy, and she ran through the woods, and she did not stop until she was safely back at home.

Little Red Riding Hood.
My Book of Favourite Fairy Tales, 1921.
Illustrated by Jenny Harbour

Little Red Riding Hood.
Old Time Stories Told by Master Charles Perrault, 1921.
Illustrated by W. Heath Robinson.

THE PANTHER

(A Chinese Tale)

The actual origins of this tale are unknown, however it most likely derived from oral traditions during the early Qing Dynasty (also known as the Manchu). The Qing were the last great imperial dynasty of China, who began their rule in 1644. This particular version was written down in *The Chinese Fairy Book* (published in 1921) by Dr. Richard Wilhelm (1873-1930), a German sinologist, theologian, and missionary. Wilhelm lived in China for twenty-five years, becoming fluent in spoken and written Chinese, as well as growing to love and admire the Chinese people and their culture.

Although a panther takes the place of the wolf in this tale, the rest of the narrative is strikingly similar to other European variants. The beast figure takes the shape of a trusted family member in order to eat the children, but meets a grizzly end analogous to Aesop's and the Grimm's narratives. Quite how *The Panther* story travelled from ancient Greece, to fourteenth century Italy and on to seventeenth century China, remains a most intriguing mystery.

$$\Longrightarrow$$

Once upon a time there was a widow who had two daughters and a little son. And one day the mother said to her daughters: "Take good care of the house, for I am going to see grandmother, together with your little brother!" So the daughters promised her they would do so, and their mother went off. On her way a panther met her, and asked where she were going.

Little Red Riding Hood.
Grimm's Fairy Tales, 1922.
Illustrated by M. L. Kirk

She said: "I am going with my child to see my mother."

"Will you not rest a bit?" asked the panther.

"No," said she, "it is already late, and it is a long road to where my mother lives."

But the panther did not cease urging her, and finally she gave in and sat down by the road side.

"I will comb your hair a bit," said the panther. And the woman allowed the panther to comb her hair. But as he passed his claws through her hair, he tore off a bit of her skin and devoured it.

"Stop!" cried the woman, "the way you comb my hair hurts!"

But the panther tore off a much larger piece of skin. Now the woman wanted to call for help, but the panther seized and devoured her. Then he turned on her little son and killed him too, put on the woman's clothes, and laid the child's bones, which he had not yet devoured, in her basket. After that he went to the woman's home, where her two daughters were, and called in at the door: "Open the door, daughters! Mother has come home!" But they looked out through a crack and said: "Our mother's eyes are not so large as yours!"

Then the panther said: "I have been to grandmother's house, and saw her hens laying eggs. That pleases me, and is the reason why my eyes have grown so large."

"Our mother had no spots in her face such as you have."

"Grandmother had no spare bed, so I had to sleep on the peas, and they pressed themselves into my face."

"Our mother's feet are not so large as yours."

"Stupid things! That comes from walking such a distance. Come, open the door quickly!"

Then the daughters said to each other: "It must be our mother," and they opened the door. But when the panther came in, they saw it was not really their mother after all.

At evening, when the daughters were already in bed, the panther was still gnawing the bones he had brought with him.

Then the daughters asked: "Mother, what are you eating?"

"I'm eating beets," was the answer.

Then the daughters said: "Oh, mother, give us some of your beets, too! We are so hungry!"

"No," was the reply, "I will not give you any. Now be quiet and go to sleep."

But the daughters kept on begging until the false mother gave them a little finger. And then they saw that it was their little brother's finger, and they said to each other: "We must make haste to escape else he will eat us as well." And with that they ran out of the door, climbed up into a tree in the yard, and called down to the false mother: "Come out! We can see our neighbor's son celebrating his wedding!" But it was the middle of the night.

Little Red Riding Hood started off at once for her Grandmother's cottage.
Little Red Riding Hood & the History of Tom Thumb, 1895.
Illustrated by H. Isabel Adams

Then the mother came out, and when she saw that they were sitting in the tree, she called out angrily: "Why, I'm not able to climb!"

The daughters said: "Get into a basket and throw us the rope and we will draw you up!"

The mother did as they said. But when the basket was half-way up, they began to swing it back and forth, and bump it against the tree. Then the false mother had to turn into a panther again, lest she fall down. And the panther leaped out of the basket, and ran away.

Gradually daylight came. The daughters climbed down, seated themselves on the doorstep, and cried for their mother. And a needle-vender came by and asked them why they were crying.

"A panther has devoured our mother and our brother," said the girls. "He has gone now, but he is sure to return and devour us as well."

Then the needle-vender gave them a pair of needles, and said: "Stick these needles in the cushion of the arm chair, with the points up." The girls thanked him and went on crying.

Soon a scorpion-catcher came by; and he asked them why they were crying. "A panther has devoured our mother and brother," said the girls. "He has gone now, but he is sure to return and devour us as well."

The man gave them a scorpion and said: "Put it behind the hearth in the kitchen." The girls thanked him and went on crying. gone now, but he is sure to return and devour us as well."

She met with Gaffer Wolf.
The Tales of Mother Goose, 1901.
Illustrated by D. J. Munro

When she got to the wood, she met a wolf.
The Fairy Tales of the Brothers Grimm, 1909.
Illustrated by Arthur Rackham

So he gave them an egg and said: "Lay it beneath the ashes in the hearth." The girls thanked him and went on crying.

Then a dealer in turtles came by, and they told him their tale. He gave them a turtle and said: "Put it in the water-barrel in the yard." And then a man came by who sold wooden clubs. He asked them why they were crying. And they told him the whole story. Then he gave them two wooden clubs and said: "Hang them up over the door to the street." The girls thanked him and did as the men had told them.

In the evening the panther came home. He sat down in the armchair in the room. Then the needles in the cushion stuck into him. So he ran into the kitchen to light the fire and see what had jabbed him so; and then it was that the scorpion hooked his sting into his hand. And when at last the fire was burning, the egg burst and spurted into one of his eyes, which was blinded. So he ran out into the yard and dipped his hand into the water-barrel, in order to cool it; and then the turtle bit it off. And when in his pain he ran out through the door into the street, the wooden clubs fell on his head and that was the end of him

He asked her whither she was going.
The Fairy Tales of Charles Perrault, 1922.
Illustrated by Harry Clarke

LITTLE RED HAT

(An Italian / Austrian Tale)

Little Red Hat, or *El Cappelin Rosso* in the Italian, and *Das Rothhütchen* in the German, is a tale collected by the Austrian philologist, poet and folklorist, Christian Schneller (1831 - 1908). It was published in his *Märchen und Sagen aus Wälschtirol: Ein Beitrag zur deutschen Sagenkunde* ('Fairy Tales and Legends from Trento: A Contribution to German Lore'), which first appeared in 1867.

Trento is a city located in the north of Italy, and was reportedly where Schneller first heard this tale. Given the multi-ethnic nature of the Austro-Hungarian Empire at the time, and the proximity of Austria's southern border to Italy, the crossover of stories is hardly surprising. *Little Red Hat* differs noticeably from the other Germanic versions (and is in fact incredibly similar to the Perrault tale, though predating it by thirty years), in that the narrative ends rather well for the wolf.

$$\Longrightarrow$$

Once there was an old woman who had a granddaughter named Little Red Hat. One day they were both in the field when the old woman said, "I am going home now. You come along later and bring me some soup."

After a while Little Red Hat set out for her grandmother's house, and she met an ogre, who said, "Hello, my dear Little Red Hat. Where are you going?"

"I am going to my grandmother's to take her some soup."

Where are you going early, Little Red Riding Hood?
My Book of Favourite Fairy Tales, 1921.
Illustrated by Jennie Harbour

26

"Good," he replied, "I'll come along too. Are you going across the stones or the thorns?"

"I'm going across the stones," said the girl.

"Then I'll go across the thorns," replied the ogre.

They left. But on the way Little Red Hat came to a meadow where beautiful flowers of all colors were in bloom, and the girl picked as many as her heart desired. Meanwhile the ogre hurried on his way, and although he had to cross the thorns, he arrived at the house before Little Red Hat. He went inside, killed the grandmother, ate her up, and climbed into her bed. He also tied her intestine onto the door in place of the latch string and placed her blood, teeth, and jaws in the kitchen cupboard.

He had barely climbed into bed when Little Red Hat arrived and knocked at the door.

"Come in" called the ogre with a dampened voice.

Little Red Hat tried to open the door, but when she noticed that she was pulling on something soft, she called out, "Grandmother, this thing is so soft!"

"Just pull and keep quiet. It is your grandmother's intestine!"

"What did you say?"

"Just pull and keep quiet!"

Little Red Hat opened the door, went inside, and said, "Grandmother, I am hungry."

The ogre replied, "Go to the kitchen cupboard. There is still a little rice there."

Little Red Hat went to the cupboard and took the teeth out. "Grandmother, these things are very hard!"

"Eat and keep quiet. They are your grandmother's teeth!"

"What did you say?"

"Eat and keep quiet!"

A little while later Little Red Hat said, "Grandmother, I'm still hungry."

"Go back to the cupboard," said the ogre. "You will find two pieces of chopped meat there."

Little Red Hat went to the cupboard and took out the jaws. "Grandmother, this is very red!"

"Eat and keep quiet. They are your grandmother's jaws!"

"What did you say?"

"Eat and keep quiet!"

A little while later Little Red Hat said, "Grandmother, I'm thirsty."

"Just look in the cupboard," said the ogre. "There must be a little wine there."

"Is it very far from hence?" asked the wolf…
The Fairy Book, 1923.
Illustrated by Warwick Goble

Little Red Hat went to the cupboard and took out the blood. "Grandmother, this wine is very red!"

"Drink and keep quiet. It is your grandmother's blood!"

"What did you say?"

"Just drink and keep quiet!"

A little while later Little Red Hat said, "Grandmother, I'm sleepy."

"Take off your clothes and get into bed with me!" replied the ogre.

Little Red Hat got into bed and noticed something hairy. "Grandmother, you are so hairy!"

"That comes with age," said the ogre.

"Grandmother, you have such long legs!"

"That comes from walking."

"Grandmother, you have such long hands!"

"That comes from working."

"Grandmother, you have such long ears!"

"That comes from listening."

"Good morning, Little Red Riding Hood," said the wolf, in a soft oily way.
Fairy Tales, 1915.
Illustrated by Margaret Tarrant

"Grandmother, you have such a big mouth!"

"That comes from eating children!" said the ogre, and bam, he swallowed Little Red Hat with one gulp.

Le Petit Chaperon Rouge.
Contes de Perrault, 1890.
Illustrated by Frédéric Théodore Lix

Red Ridinghood.
A Child's Book of Stories, 1914.
Illustrated by Jessie Willcox Smith

Le Petit Chaperon Rouge

(A French Tale)

This version was penned by Charles Perrault (1628-1703), a French author and member of the Académie Française – a man largely responsible for laying the foundations of the fairy-tale genre.

Le Petit Chaperon Rouge was published in 1697, in *Histoires ou Contes du Temps Passé: Les Contes de ma Mère l'Oye* ('Tales and Stories of the Past with Morals: Tales of Mother Goose'). All of Perrault's works were based on pre-existing stories, but his flair for storytelling 'fixed' the narrative as we know it today. As the title of the collection implies, Perrault's version of *Little Red Riding Hood* is both more sinister and more overtly moralized than many earlier tales. The redness of the hood, which has been given symbolic significance in many interpretations of the story, was a detail introduced by Perrault.

Once upon a time, there lived in a certain village, a little country girl, the prettiest creature was ever seen. Her mother was excessively fond of her; and her grand-mother doted on her much more. This good woman got made for her a little red riding-hood; which became the girl so extremely well, that every body called her Little Red Riding-Hood.

One day, her mother, having made some girdle-cakes, said to her:

"Go, my dear, and see how thy grand-mamma does, for I hear she has been very ill, carry her a girdle-cake, and this little pot of butter."

35

Le Petit Chaperon Rouge.
Les Contes Des Fees, 1908.
Illustrated by M. M. Parquet

Little Red Riding-Hood set out immediately to go to her grand-mother, who lived in another village. As she was going thro' the wood, she met with Gaffer Wolf, who had a very great mind to eat her up, but he durst not, because of some faggot-makers hard by in the forest.

He asked her whither she was going. The poor child, who did not know that it was dangerous to stay and hear a Wolf talk, said to him:

"I am going to see my grand-mamma, and carry her a girdle-cake, and a little pot of butter, from my mamma."

"Does she live far off?" said the Wolf.

"Oh! ay," answered Little Red Riding-Hood, "it is beyond that mill you see there, at the first house in the village."

"Well," said the Wolf, "and I'll go and see her too: I'll go this way, and you go that, and we shall see who will be there soonest."

The Wolf began to run as fast as he could, taking the nearest way; and the little girl went by that farthest about, diverting herself in gathering nuts, running after butterflies, and making nosegays of such little flowers as she met with. The Wolf was not long before he got to the old woman's house: he knocked at the door, *tap, tap*.

"Who's there?"

"Your grand-child, Little Red Riding-Hood," replied the Wolf, counterfeiting her voice, "who has brought you a girdle-cake, and a little pot of butter, sent you by mamma."

The good grand-mother, who was in bed, because she found herself somewhat ill, cry'd out:

"Pull the peg, and the bolt will fall."

The Wolf pull'd the peg, and the door opened, and then presently he fell upon the good woman, and ate her up in a moment; for it was above three days that he had not touched a bit. He then shut the door, and went into the grand-mother's bed, expecting Little Red Riding-Hood, who came some time afterwards, and knock'd at the door, *tap, tap.*

"Who's there?"

Little Red Riding-Hood, hearing the big voice of the Wolf, was at first afraid; but believing her grand-mother had got a cold, and was hoarse, answered:

"'Tis your grand-child, Little Red Riding-Hood, who has brought you a girdle-cake, and a little pot of butter, mamma sends you."

The Wolf cried out to her, softening his voice as much as he could, "Pull the peg, and the bolt will fall."

Little Red Riding-Hood pulled the peg, and the door opened. The Wolf seeing her come in, said to her, hiding himself under the bedclothes:

"Put the cake, and the little pot of butter upon the bread-bin, and come and lye down with me."

Little Red Riding-Hood undressed herself, and went into bed; where, being greatly amazed to see how her grand-mother looked in her night-clothes, she said to her:

Little Red Riding Hood.
The Big Book of Fairy Tales, 1911.
Illustrated by Charles Robinson

*She couldn't even pass a puddle without peeping down
into it at her apple cheeks and yellow hair.*

Little Red Riding Hood, 1927.

Illustrated by A. H. Watson

"Grand-mamma, what great arms you have got!"

"That is the better to hug thee, my dear."

"Grand-mamma, what great legs you have got!"

"That is to run the better, my child."

"Grand-mamma, what great ears you have got!"

"That is to hear the better, my child."

"Grand-mamma, what great eyes you have got!"

"It is to see the better, my child."

"Grand-mamma, what great teeth you have got!"

"That is to eat thee up."

And, saying these words, this wicked Wolf fell upon poor Little Red Riding-Hood, and ate her all up.

The Moral

From this short story easy we discern
What conduct all young people ought to learn.
But above all, young, growing misses fair,
Whose orient rosy blooms begin t'appear:
Who, beauties in the fragrant spring of age,
With pretty airs young hearts are apt t'engage.
Ill do they listen to all sorts of tongues,
Since some inchant and lure like Syrens' songs.
No wonder therefore 'tis, if over-power'd,
So many of them has the Wolf devour'd.
The Wolf, I say, for Wolves too sure there are
Of every sort, and every character.
Some of them mild and gentle-humour'd be,
Of noise and gall, and rancour wholly free;
Who tame, familiar, full of complaisance
Ogle and leer, languish, cajole and glance;
With luring tongues, and language wond'rous sweet,
Follow young ladies as they walk the street,
Ev'n to their very houses, nay, bedside,
And, artful, tho' their true designs they hide;
Yet ah! these simpering Wolves! Who does not see
Most dangerous of Wolves indeed they be?

They are looking at me as I go along in my bright red hood.
Told Again - Old Tales Told Again, 1927.
Illustration by A. H. Watson

He fell upon the good woman.
The Tales of Mother Goose, 1901.
Illustrated by D. J. Munro

ROTKÄPPCHEN

(A German Tale)

Rotkäppchen ('Little Red Cap') is a German tale written by the Brothers Grimm, (or *Die Brüder Grimm*), Jacob (1785–1863) and Wilhelm Grimm (1786–1859). It was published in *Kinder und Hausmärchen* ('Children's and Household Tales') in 1812; a pioneering collection of German folklore. The Grimms built their anthology on the conviction that a national identity could be found in popular culture and with the common folk (*Volk*). Their first volumes were highly criticised however, because although they were called 'Children's Tales', they were not regarded as suitable for children, for both their scholarly information and gruesome subject matter.

The story of *Rotkäppchen* was told to the brothers by Jeanette Hassenpflug (1791-1860) and the earlier parts of the narrative agree so closely with Perrault's variant that it is almost certainly the source of the tale. The Grimms modified the ending however, and this account has the little girl and her grandmother saved by a huntsman who was after the wolf's skin; an identical conclusion to that in *The Wolf and the Seven Young Kids*, which appears to be the source.

➤——→

Once upon a time there was a dear little girl who was loved by every one who looked at her, but most of all by her grandmother, and there was nothing that she would not have given to the child. Once she gave her a little cap of red velvet, which suited her so well that she would never wear anything else; so she was always called "Little Red-Cap."

Without a word he jumped on to the bed and gobbled up the poor old lady.
My Book of Favourite Fairy Tales, 1921.

Illustrated by Jennie Harbour

One day her mother said to her, "Come, Little Red-Cap, here is a piece of cake and a bottle of wine; take them to your grandmother, she is ill and weak, and they will do her good. Set out before it gets hot, and when you are going, walk nicely and quietly and do not run off the path, or you may fall and break the bottle, and then your grandmother will get nothing; and when you go into her room, don't forget to say, 'Good-morning,' and don't peep into every corner before you do it."

"I will take great care," said Little Red-Cap to her mother, and gave her hand on it.

The grandmother lived out in the wood, half a league from the village, and just as Little Red-Cap entered the wood, a wolf met her. Red-Cap did not know what a wicked creature he was, and was not at all afraid of him.

"Good-day, Little Red-Cap," said he.

"Thank you kindly, wolf."

"Whither away so early, Little Red-Cap?"

"To my grandmother's."

"What have you got in your apron?"

"Cake and wine; yesterday was baking-day, so poor sick grandmother is to have something good, to make her stronger."

"Where does your grandmother live, Little Red-Cap?"

"A good quarter of a league farther on in the wood; her house stands under the three large oak-trees, the nut-trees are just below; you surely must know it," replied Little Red-Cap.

The wolf thought to himself, "What a tender young creature! what a nice plump mouthful -- she will be better to eat than the old woman. I must act craftily, so as to catch both." So he walked for a short time by the side of Little Red-Cap, and then he said, "See Little Red-Cap, how pretty the flowers are about here -- why do you not look round? I believe, too, that you do not hear how sweetly the little birds are singing; you walk gravely along as if you were going to school, while everything else out here in the wood is merry."

Little Red-Cap raised her eyes, and when she saw the sunbeams dancing here and there through the trees, and pretty flowers growing everywhere, she thought, "Suppose I take grandmother a fresh nosegay; that would please her too. It is so early in the day that I shall still get there in good time;" and so she ran from the path into the wood to look for flowers. And whenever she had picked one, she fancied that she saw a still prettier one farther on, and ran after it, and so got deeper and deeper into the wood.

Meanwhile the wolf ran straight to the grandmother's house and knocked at the door.

"Who is there?"

"Little Red-Cap," replied the wolf. "She is bringing cake and wine; open the door."

"Lift the latch," called out the grandmother, "I am too weak, and cannot get up."

She came knocking at the door.
Little Red Riding Hood & the History of Tom Thumb, 1895.
Illustrated by H. Isabel Adams

Red Riding Hood tripped into the room, fresh and dainty with her walk.
Fairy Tales, 1915.
Illustrated by Margaret Tarrant

The wolf lifted the latch, the door flew open, and without saying a word he went straight to the grandmother's bed, and devoured her. Then he put on her clothes, dressed himself in her cap, laid himself in bed and drew the curtains.

Little Red-Cap, however, had been running about picking flowers, and when she had gathered so many that she could carry no more, she remembered her grandmother, and set out on the way to her.

She was surprised to find the cottage-door standing open, and when she went into the room, she had such a strange feeling that she said to herself, "Oh dear! how uneasy I feel to-day, and at other times I like being with grandmother so much." She called out, "Good morning," but received no answer; so she went to the bed and drew back the curtains. There lay her grandmother with her cap pulled far over her face, and looking very strange.

"Oh! grandmother," she said, "what big ears you have!"

"The better to hear you with, my child," was the reply.

"But, grandmother, what big eyes you have!" she said.

"The better to see you with, my dear."

"But, grandmother, what large hands you have!"

"The better to hug you with."

"Oh! but, grandmother, what a terrible big mouth you have!"

"The better to eat you with!"

And scarcely had the wolf said this, than with one bound he was out of bed and swallowed up Red-Cap.

When the wolf had appeased his appetite, he lay down again in the bed, fell asleep and began to snore very loud. The huntsman was just passing the house, and thought to himself, "How the old woman is snoring! I must just see if she wants anything." So he went into the room, and when he came to the bed, he saw that the wolf was lying in it. "Do I find thee here, thou old sinner!" said he. "I have long sought thee!" Then just as he was going to fire at him, it occurred to him that the wolf might have devoured the grandmother, and that she might still be saved, so he did not fire, but took a pair of scissors, and began to cut open the stomach of the sleeping wolf. When he had made two snips, he saw the little Red-Cap shining, and then he made two snips more, and the little girl sprang out, crying, "Ah, how frightened I have been! How dark it was inside the wolf;" and after that the aged grandmother came out alive also, but scarcely able to breathe. Red-Cap, however, quickly fetched great stones with which they filled the wolf's body, and when he awoke, he wanted to run away, but the stones were so heavy that he fell down at once, and fell dead.

Then all three were delighted. The huntsman drew off the wolf's skin and went home with it; the grandmother ate the cake and drank the wine which Red-Cap had brought, and revived, but Red-Cap thought to herself, "As long as I live, I will never by myself leave the path, to run into the wood, when my mother has forbidden me to do so."

I've come all the way by myself in my new red riding-hood.
Told Again - Old Tales Told Again, 1927.
Illustration by A. H. Watson

"O Grandmother, what big ears you have got," she said.
The Fairy Tales of the Brothers Grimm, 1909.
Illustrated by Arthur Rackham

THE TRUE STORY OF
LITTLE GOLDEN HOOD

(A British Tale)

The True Story of Little Golden Hood was propagated by the Scottish folklorist Andrew Lang (1844 - 1912), in *The Red Fairy Book* (1890). Lang produced twelve collections of fairy tales in total, each volume distinguished by its own colour. Although he did not collect the stories himself from oral-tellings, Lang is only rivalled by Madame d'Aulnoy (1650 - 1705) for the sheer variety of sources and cultural diversity included in his anthologies.

This particular version is thought to have come from the French folklorist Charles Marelles, in the *Contes de Charles Marelles*. Lang was concerned that the graphic nature of the violence was unfit for younger readers, and so explicitly stated that the story had been mis-told earlier. Such bowdlerising is classic of this late Victorian period, and is in itself an intriguing development in the tale's evolution. In the following story, Little Golden Hood's salvation comes not from the huntsman, but from her extraordinary garment.

$$\longrightarrow$$

You know the tale of poor Little Red Riding-hood, that the Wolf deceived and devoured, with her cake, her little butter can, and her Grandmother; well, the true story happened quite differently, as we know now. And first of all the little girl was called and is still called Little Golden-hood; secondly, it was not she, nor the good grand-dame, but the wicked Wolf who was, in the end, caught and devoured.

Only listen.

The story begins something like the tale.

There was once a little peasant girl, pretty and nice as a star in its season. Her real name was Blanchette, but she was more often called Little Golden-hood, on account of a wonderful little cloak with a hood, gold-and fire-coloured, which she always had on. This little hood was given her by her Grandmother, who was so old that she did not know her age; it ought to bring her good luck, for it was made of a ray of sunshine, she said. And as the good old woman was considered something of a witch, everyone thought the little hood rather bewitched too.

And so it was, as you will see.

One day the mother said to the child: 'Let us see, my little Golden-hood, if you know now how to find your way by yourself. You shall take this good piece of cake to your Grandmother for a Sunday treat to-morrow. You will ask her how she is, and come back at once, without stopping to chatter on the way with people you don't know. Do you quite understand?'

'I quite understand,' replied Blanchette gaily. And off she went with the cake, quite proud of her errand.

But the Grandmother lived in another village, and there was a big wood to cross before getting there. At a turn of the road under the trees, suddenly 'Who goes there?'

'Friend Wolf.'

How queer your voice is, Grandmother!
The Now-A-Days Fairy Book, 1922.
Illustrated by Jessie Willcox Smith

He had seen the child start alone, and the villain was waiting to devour her; when at the same moment he perceived some wood-cutters who might observe him, and he changed his mind. Instead of falling upon Blanchette he came frisking up to her like a good dog.

' 'Tis you! my nice Little Golden-hood,' said he. So the little girl stops to talk with the Wolf, who, for all that, she did not know in the least.

'You know me, then!' said she; 'what is your name?'

'My name is friend Wolf. And where are you going thus, my pretty one, with your little basket on your arm?'

'I am going to my Grandmother, to take her a good piece of cake for her Sunday treat to-morrow.'

'And where does she live, your Grandmother?'

'She lives at the other side of the wood, in the first house in the village, near the windmill, you know.'

'Ah! yes! I know now,' said the Wolf. 'Well, that's just where I'm going; I shall get there before you, no doubt, with your little bits of legs, and I'll tell her you're coming to see her; then she'll wait for you.'

Thereupon the Wolf cuts across the wood, and in five minutes arrives at the Grandmother's house.

He knocks at the door: toc, toc.

No answer.

Grandmother, grandmother, what great eyes you've got.
Nursery Tales, 1923.

Illustrated by Paul Woodroffe

Grandma what great ears you have.
Tales of Passed Times, 1900.
Illustrated by Charles Robinson

He knocks louder.

Nobody.

Then he stands up on end, puts his two fore-paws on the latch and the door opens.

Not a soul in the house.

The old woman had risen early to sell herbs in the town, and she had gone off in such haste that she had left her bed unmade, with her great night-cap on the pillow.

'Good!' said the Wolf to himself, 'I know what I'll do.'

He shuts the door, pulls on the Grandmother's night-cap down to his eyes, then he lies down all his length in the bed and draws the curtains.

In the meantime the good Blanchette went quietly on her way, as little girls do, amusing herself here and there by picking Easter daisies, watching the little birds making their nests, and running after the butterflies which fluttered in the sunshine.

At last she arrives at the door.

Knock, knock.

'Who is there?' says the Wolf, softening his rough voice as best he can.

'It's me, Granny, your little Golden-hood. I'm bringing you a big piece of cake for your Sunday treat to-morrow.'

'Press your finger on the latch, then push and the door opens.'

'Why, you've got a cold, Granny,' said she, coming in.

'Ahem! a little, a little . . .' replies the Wolf, pretending to cough. 'Shut the door well, my little lamb. Put your basket on the table, and then take off your frock and come and lie down by me: you shall rest a little.'

The good child undresses, but observe this! She kept her little hood upon her head. When she saw what a figure her Granny cut in bed, the poor little thing was much surprised.

'Oh!' cries she, 'how like you are to friend Wolf, Grandmother!'

'That's on account of my night-cap, child,' replies the Wolf.

'Oh! what hairy arms you've got, Grandmother!'

'All the better to hug you, my child.'

'Oh! what a big tongue you've got, Grandmother!'

'All the better for answering, child.'

'Oh! what a mouthful of great white teeth you have, Grandmother!'

'That's for crunching little children with! 'And the Wolf opened his jaws wide to swallow Blanchette.

But she put down her head crying:

"What a terrible large mouth you have got!"
Grimm's Fairy Tales, 1917.
Illustrated by Louis Rhead

"But, Grandmother, what a horrible large mouth you have!" "The better to eat you!"
Grimm's Fairy Tales, 1911.
Illustrated by Charles Folkard

'Mamma! Mamma!' and the Wolf only caught her little hood.

Thereupon, oh dear! oh dear! he draws back, crying and shaking his jaw as if he had swallowed red-hot coals.

It was the little fire-coloured hood that had burnt his tongue right down his throat.

The little hood, you see, was one of those magic caps that they used to have in former times, in the stories, for making oneself invisible or invulnerable.

So there was the Wolf with his throat burnt, jumping off the bed and trying to find the door, howling and howling as if all the dogs in the country were at his heels.

Just at this moment the Grandmother arrives, returning from the town with her long sack empty on her shoulder.

'Ah, brigand!' she cries, 'wait a bit!' Quickly she opens her sack wide across the door, and the maddened Wolf springs in head downwards.

It is he now that is caught, swallowed like a letter in the post.

For the brave old dame shuts her sack, so; and she runs and empties it in the well, where the vagabond, still howling, tumbles in and is drowned.

'Ah, scoundrel! you thought you would crunch my little grandchild! Well, to-morrow we will make her a muff of your skin, and you yourself shall be crunched, for we will give your carcass to the dogs.'

Thereupon the Grandmother hastened to dress poor Blanchette, who was still trembling with fear in the bed.

'Well,' she said to her, 'without my little hood where would you be now, darling?' And, to restore heart and legs to the child, she made her eat a good piece of her cake, and drink a good draught of wine, after which she took her by the hand and led her back to the house.

And then, who was it who scolded her when she knew all that had happened?

It was the mother.

But Blanchette promised over and over again that she would never more stop to listen to a Wolf, so that at last the mother forgave her.

And Blanchette, the Little Golden-hood, kept her word. And in fine weather she may still be seen in the fields with her pretty little hood, the colour of the sun.

But to see her you must rise early.

He draws back, crying and shaking his jaw as if he had swallowed red-hot coals.
The Red Fairy Book, 1890.
Illustrated by Lancelot Speed

THE GOLDEN AGE OF ILLUSTRATION

The 'Golden age of Illustration' refers to a period customarily defined as lasting from the latter quarter of the nineteenth century until just after the First World War. In this period of no more than fifty years the popularity, abundance and most importantly the unprecedented upsurge in quality of illustrated works marked an astounding change in the way that publishers, artists and the general public came to view this hitherto insufficiently esteemed art form.

Until the latter part of the nineteenth century, the work of illustrators was largely proffered anonymously, and in England it was only after Thomas Bewick's pioneering technical advances in wood engraving that it became common to acknowledge the artistic and technical expertise of book and magazine illustrators. Although widely regarded as the patriarch of the *Golden Age*, Walter Crane (1845-1915) started his career as an anonymous illustrator – gradually building his reputation through striking designs, famous for their sharp outlines and flat tints of colour. Like many other great illustrators to follow, Crane operated within many different mediums; a lifelong disciple of William Morris and a member of the Arts and Crafts Movement, he designed all manner of objects including wallpaper, furniture, ceramic ware and even whole interiors. This incredibly important and inclusive phase of British design proved to have a lasting impact on illustration both in the United Kingdom and Europe as well as America.

The artists involved in the Arts and Crafts Movement attempted to counter the ever intruding Industrial Revolution (the first wave of which lasted roughly from 1750-1850) by bringing the values of beautiful and inventive craftsmanship back into the sphere of everyday life. It must be noted that around the turn of the century the boundaries between what would today be termed 'fine art' as opposed to 'crafts' and 'design' were far more fluid and in many cases non-operational, and many illustrators had lucrative painterly careers in addition to their design work. The Romanticism of the *Pre Raphaelite Brotherhood* combined with the intricate curvatures of the *Art Nouveaux* movement provided influential strands running through most illustrators work. The latter especially so for the Scottish illustrator Anne Anderson (1874-1930) as well as the Dutch artist Kay Nielson (1886-1957), who was also inspired by the stunning work of Japanese artists such as Hiroshige.

One of the main accomplishments of nineteenth century illustration lay in its ability to reach far wider numbers than the traditional 'high arts'. In 1892 the American critic William A. Coffin praised the new medium for popularising art; 'more has been done through the medium of illustrated literature... to make the masses of people realise that there is such a thing as art and that it is worth caring about'. Commercially, illustrated publications reached their zenith with the burgeoning 'Gift Book' industry which emerged in the first decade of the twentieth century. The first widely distributed gift book was published in 1905. It comprised of Washington Irving's short story *Rip Van Winkle* with the addition of 51 colour plates by a true master of illustration; Arthur Rackham. Rackham created each plate by first painstakingly drawing his subject in a sinuous pencil line before applying an ink layer – then he used layer upon layer of delicate watercolours to build up the romantic yet calmly ethereal results on which his reputation was constructed. Although Rackham is now one of the most recognisable names in illustration, his delicate palette owed no small debt to Kate Greenaway (1846-1901) – one of the first female illustrators whose pioneering and incredibly subtle use of the watercolour medium resulted in her election to the Royal Institute of Painters in Water Colours in 1889.

The year before Arthur Rackam's illustrations for *Rip Van Winkle* were published, a young and aspiring French artist by the name of Edmund Dulac (1882-1953) came to London and was to create a similarly impressive legacy. His timing could not have been more fortuitous. Several factors converged around the turn of the century which allowed illustrators and publishers alike a far greater freedom of creativity than previously imagined. The origination of the 'colour separation' practice meant that colour images, extremely faithful to the original artwork could be produced on a grand scale. Dulac possessed a rigorously painterly background (more so than his contemporaries) and was hence able to utilise the new technology so as to allow the colour itself to refine and define an object as opposed to the traditional pen and ink line. It has been estimated that in 1876 there was only one 'colour separation' firm in London, but by 1900 this number had rocketed to fifty. This improvement in printing quality also meant a reduction in labour, and coupled with the introduction of new presses and low-cost supplies of paper this meant that publishers could for the first time afford to pay high wages for highly talented artists.

Whilst still in the U.K, no survey of the *Golden Age of Illustration* would be complete without a mention of the Heath-Robinson brothers. Charles Robinson was renowned for his beautifully detached style, whether in pen and ink or sumptuous watercolours. Whilst William (the youngest) was to later garner immense fame for his carefully constructed yet tortuous machines operated by comical, intensely serious attendants. After World War One the Robinson brothers numbered among the few artists of the Golden Age who continued to regularly produce illustrated works. As we move towards the United States, one illustrator - Howard Pyle (1853-1911) stood head and shoulders above his contemporaries as the most distinguished illustrator of the age. From 1880 onwards Pyle illustrated over 100 volumes, yet it was not quantity which ensured his precedence over other American (and European) illustrators, but quality.

Pyle's sumptuous illustrations benefitted from a meticulous composition process livened with rich colour and deep recesses, providing a visual framework in which tales such as *Robin Hood* and *The Four Volumes of the Arthurian Cycle* could come to life. These are publications which remain continuous good sellers up till the present day. His flair and originality combined with a thoroughness of planning and execution were principles which he passed onto his many pupils at the *Drexel Institute of Arts and Sciences*. Two such pupils were Jessie Willcox Smith (1863-1935) who went on to illustrate books such as *The Water Babies* and *At the Back of North Wind* and perhaps most famously Maxfield Parrish (1870-1966) who became famed for luxurious colour (most remarkably demonstrated in his blue paintings) and imaginative designs; practices in no short measure gleaned from his tutor. As an indication of Parrish's popularity, in 1925 it was estimated that one fifth of American households possessed a Parrish reproduction.

As is evident from this brief introduction to the 'Golden Age of Illustration', it was a period of massive technological change and artistic ingenuity. The legacy of this enormously important epoch lives on in the present day – in the continuing popularity and respect afforded to illustrators, graphic and fine artists alike. This *Origins of Fairy Tales from Around the World* series will hopefully provide a fascinating insight into an era of intense historical and creative development, bringing both little known stories, and the art that has accompanied them, back to life.

OTHER TITLES IN THE 'ORIGINS OF FAIRY TALES FROM AROUND THE WORLD' SERIES...

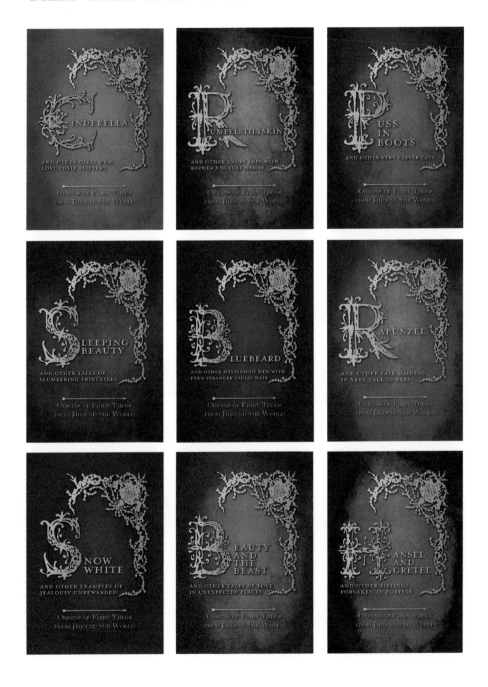

CINDERELLA

AND OTHER GIRLS WHO
LOST THEIR SLIPPERS

ORIGINS OF FAIRY TALES
FROM AROUND THE WORLD

RUMPELSTILTSKIN

AND OTHER ANGRY IMPS WITH
RATHER UNUSUAL NAMES

ORIGINS OF FAIRY TALES
FROM AROUND THE WORLD

PUSS IN BOOTS

AND OTHER VERY CLEVER CATS

ORIGINS OF FAIRY TALES
FROM AROUND THE WORLD

SLEEPING BEAUTY

AND OTHER TALES OF
SLUMBERING PRINCESSES

ORIGINS OF FAIRY TALES
FROM AROUND THE WORLD

BLUEBEARD

AND OTHER MYSTERIOUS MEN WITH
EVEN STRANGER FACIAL HAIR

ORIGINS OF FAIRY TALES
FROM AROUND THE WORLD

RAPUNZEL

AND OTHER FAIR MAIDENS
IN VERY TALL TOWERS

ORIGINS OF FAIRY TALES
FROM AROUND THE WORLD

SNOW WHITE

AND OTHER EXAMPLES OF
JEALOUSY UNREWARDED

ORIGINS OF FAIRY TALES
FROM AROUND THE WORLD

BEAUTY AND THE BEAST

AND OTHER TALES OF LOVE
IN UNEXPECTED PLACES

ORIGINS OF FAIRY TALES
FROM AROUND THE WORLD

HANSEL AND GRETEL

AND OTHER SIBLINGS
FORSAKEN IN FORESTS

ORIGINS OF FAIRY TALES
FROM AROUND THE WORLD

Printed in Great Britain
by Amazon

79130339R00047